THOMAS
AND THE CASTLE

Illustrated by Tommy Stubbs

Random House New York

Thomas the Tank Engine & Friends®

A BRITT ALLCROFT COMPANY PRODUCTION
Based on The Railway Series by The Reverend W Awdry. © 2004 Gullane (Thomas) LLC.
Thomas the Tank Engine & Friends and Thomas & Friends are trademarks of Gullane Entertainment Inc.
Thomas the Tank Engine & Friends is Reg. U.S. Pat. TM Off.

A HIT Entertainment Company

www.randomhouse.com/kids/thomas   www.thomasthetankengine.com

Library of Congress Cataloging-in-Publication Data
Thomas and the castle / illustrated by Tommy Stubbs. p.   cm. — (Thomas & friends)
"Based on the Railway Series by the Rev. W. Awdry."
SUMMARY: When Percy and the others report seeing ghosts at Rolf's Castle, Thomas takes a look for himself.
ISBN 0-375-81393-4 (trade)
[1. Railroads—Trains—Fiction. 2. Ghosts—Fiction.] I. Stubbs, Tommy, ill. II. Awdry W. III. Awdry, W. Railway series.
IV. Series   PZ7.T3694 5942 2004   [E]—dc22 2004005782

Printed in the United States of America   First Edition   10 9 8 7 6 5 4 3 2

It was a fine fall morning on the Island of Sodor, and Thomas was looking forward to pulling coaches on his branch line. But Percy was telling ghost stories. "My driver saw the *ghost train* last night. They say that it appears to engines once in a while as a warning of trouble ahead."

"Pooh," said Thomas. "Silly Percy! Really Useful Engines don't have time for ghost stories. *I'm* not scared."

The next evening, Percy was coming home from the harbor. He was humming along the rails, almost to Crowe's Farm Crossing.

Little did Percy know that a cart of flour was stuck on the tracks at the crossing!

Percy came upon the cart swiftly in the dark. He smashed it to smithereens in a billowing cloud of white flour!

When the dust cleared, Percy was a ghostly white. "Whew," said his driver. "I'm glad no one was hurt, Percy. But you look like a ghost. Let's go get you a washdown."

"Let me stay this way," said Percy. "I think I know someone who deserves a good scare!"

On the way home, Percy came upon Toby and convinced him to help scare Thomas. Toby pulled into the yard first and told Thomas, "Percy's had an accident!" Just then, ghostly Percy rolled up, making an awful moaning and clanking sound. Thomas was so scared, he hurried out of the yard.

Percy and Toby had a good laugh. "That will teach Thomas to say I'm a silly engine," said Percy with a smile.

Thomas soon figured out that Percy was only fooling about being a ghost. And a couple of days later, when James came home with another scary story, Thomas thought the other engines were still playing tricks on him.

"I saw spooky lights floating around Rolf's Castle tonight," said James.

"But that castle has been abandoned for years," said Gordon.

"Maybe it's a ghost," guessed Percy.

"Pish posh," said Thomas. "You won't fool me again."

A week went by, and Thomas forgot about silly ghost stories . . . until he met Bill and Ben at the crossing one morning. "Thomas, you won't believe what we saw last night!" said Bill.

"There were ghosts inside Rolf's Castle," said Ben.

"Spooky," said Bill.

"Creepy," said Ben.

"And then," said Bill, "the signal was green when it should have been red. I almost crashed into Ben."

"Spooky," said Ben.

"Creepy," said Bill.

Thomas thought that Bill and Ben were probably just teasing, but he was still uneasy. He asked Sir Topham Hatt for routes that would take him far from Rolf's Castle. As he was getting ready to take some Troublesome Trucks to the mine, Gordon came chugging up.

"Thomas, why are you going to the mine?" asked Gordon. "Are you afraid of Rolf's Castle?"

"I'm not afraid of anything," wheeshed Thomas. And he chuffed away.

"I'll show him," said
Thomas.
"Scaredy-cat. Scaredy-cat,"
sang the trucks.

Thomas didn't know it, but the mines were a dangerous place. Long ago, miners had made tunnels, and some of their roofs were not strong enough to hold up an engine, even one as small as Thomas. There were danger signs everywhere.

But Thomas was still stung by Gordon's and the trucks' taunts. *I'm not afraid of a silly old sign,* thought Thomas.

To prove he wasn't afraid, Thomas bumped some empty trucks fiercely, sending them right through a sign and onto the siding beyond. Thomas foolishly followed the trucks right onto the dangerous siding. "Hurrah," laughed Thomas. "There's nothing to be scared of!"

Just then, the rails started to quiver. The track gave way, and Thomas sank into the mine!

Gordon had to be sent to pull Thomas out of the hole. "Thanks, Gordon," said Thomas. "I was just trying to prove I wasn't scared of anything."

"That's okay," said Gordon. "I'm sorry I made fun of you."

Thomas decided that being foolish was not the same as being
brave. So when Sir Topham Hatt needed an engine to pull a Special
right to Rolf's Castle, Thomas volunteered. He wanted to be a
Really Useful Engine.

As Thomas started off for the castle, night was falling and fog was rolling in. Thomas was very afraid, but he chugged on bravely. Ahead in the fog, he saw an eerie glow. *It's a ghost!* he thought. *Just like the one James saw.*

But as Thomas came up the hill, a brisk wind blew and the fog cleared. Thomas saw that there was no ghost at all. It was just the fog man with his lantern. Thomas realized that James hadn't seen a ghost after all. Just lanterns in the fog. But what were lanterns doing in an abandoned castle?

Although the fog had blown away, the moon was still behind the clouds. When Thomas saw something white fluttering up ahead, he was *sure* it was the ghost this time! "Don't be scared, don't be scared," he huffed to himself.

Thomas chugged bravely on and realized that the fluttering white thing was . . . *curtains! Well, bust my boiler,* Thomas thought. *Maybe the ghosts Bill and Ben saw were just curtains. What is going on here?* It was all a mystery.

When Thomas approached the signal near the castle, it was flashing red, then green, then red again. "That's funny," said Thomas to the signalman. "Bill and Ben were having problems with this same signal the other night."

But Thomas wasn't scared anymore. He thought he might have an idea what was going on at the castle. He asked the signalman, "Are there people moving into the castle?"

"No, but your guess is close," said the signalman. "They are restoring the castle. And the electrical work they are doing has been causing my signal to go haywire. But, Thomas, you'd better move on . . . they're expecting that load you're pulling."

When Thomas finally arrived at Rolf's Castle, Sir Topham Hatt was there, getting ready for a big party to celebrate the reopening of the castle!

Thomas was relieved that there was nothing to be scared of after all. He was also proud to have figured out the mystery. "Thomas," said Sir Topham Hatt, "you have been brave and clever. You are a Really Useful Engine."